ROMPING MONSTERS, STOMPING MONSTERS

JANE YOLEN

illustrated by KELLY MURPHY

CANDLEWICK PRESS

First edition 2013

Library of Congress Catalog Card Number 2012943655
ISBN 978-0-7636-5727-7

13 14 15 16 17 18 LEO 10 9 8 7 6 5 4 3 2 1

Printed in Heshan, Guangdong, China

This book was typeset in Wilke Bold.
The illustrations were done in oil, acrylic, and gel medium on paper.

Candlewick Press
99 Dover Street
Somerville, Massachusetts 02144

visit us at www.candlewick.com

For Ella and Anna MacLachlan,
who borrowed my house the summer of 2012.
Hope you found enough books.
Here's one more.
J. Y.

For Antoine and his monsterly advice
K. M.

Monsters stretch.
Monsters twirl.

Monsters catch.

Monsters hurl.

Monsters tumble,
Run, and lope.

Monsters jump
A monster rope.

Monsters hopscotch.

Monsters slide.

Monsters swing
And piggy-back ride.

Monsters in
Three-legged races

Fall upon
Their monster faces.

Monsters teeter,

Monsters totter,

Monsters faces
Red and hotter.

Monsters clap
And laugh and tickle.

Monsters eat
A monster-sicle.

Want a drink.

Say you're sorry.

All better now.